W9-CEI-142

Attention,
all Super Hero Squad fans!
Look for these items when you read this book.
Can you guess which of your favorite
characters use them?

HELMET

IRON GLOVE

HORNS

HEADQUARTERS

Little, Brown and Company • Hachette Book Group • 237 Park Avenue, New York, NY
10017 • Visit our website at www.lb-kids.com • LB kids is an imprint of Little, Brown
and Company. The LB kids name and logo are trademarks of Hachette Book Group, Inc.

First edition: September 2010 • 10 9 8 7 6 5 4 3 2 1

ISBN: 978-0-316-08484-0
CW
Printed in the United States of America

MEET THE VILLAINS OF VILLAINVILLE

by Lucy Rosen
illustrated by Dario Brizuela

LITTLE, BROWN & COMPANY
LB kids

The Super Hero Squad
protects Super Hero City,
watching over it from
the Squad's flying headquarters.

It is up to the Super Heroes
to keep their city safe from villains.

Across the river
from Super Hero City
is a dark and scary place.
It is called Villainville.

The skies are always stormy
in Villainville.
The homes need to be fixed,
and no one cares about the rules.

The bad guys who live
in Villainville
have one mission.

They want to make trouble
for all the heroes in
Super Hero City!

Dr. Doom is the leader
of this band of evildoers.
From his secret lair,
he gives the villains their orders.

He rules with an iron fist
and an army of robot Sentinels.
Now he wants to rule the world.
If only the Squaddies
would stay out of his way!

Magneto is the master of magnetism.
He can move anything made of metal.

But Magneto sometimes gets upset.
Metal objects can stick to him
when he does not want them!
Even superpowers can go wrong!

Super Skrull has many superpowers!
He can control fire,
generate force fields,
and become invisible.

He can also stretch superlong
and make his skin rock hard.
Skrull is like four villains in one!
He is Villainville's
most dangerous bad guy.

Loki creates mayhem
wherever he goes.
He plays magical pranks
on all the Super Heroes.

Loki's favorite hero to annoy is his half brother, Thor!

Mystique likes to play
tricks of her own.

With skin that can change
size and shape,
this sly villain can be anyone's twin.
It makes her hard to catch!

Doc Ock's extra mechanical arms
make it easy for him to cause trouble.

The Super Heroes must be fast
if they want to catch Doc Ock.
He escapes by crawling away
in no time!

Don't mess with Abomination!
He is one of the strongest guys around.

Abomination uses his mutated size
to destroy everything in sight.
He is Villainville's biggest bully.

ONE WAY

When the Super Villains
need a little extra help,
they call on their army of robots.

The Sentinels can zoom through the air
and use cables to capture the heroes.
One thing is certain:
These fighting machines mean business!

The good guys in
Super Hero City
are brave, strong, and tough.

But these awful villains
are planning to give them a fight
the Super Heroes won't forget.

"Ready to attack the Super Hero Squad?" yells Dr. Doom to his gang of evil warriors.

"Ready!" scream the Super Villains.

This will be the biggest battle ever!
Who will win?